MY BOOK

Nursery Tales

CONTENTS

Marshall Cavendish

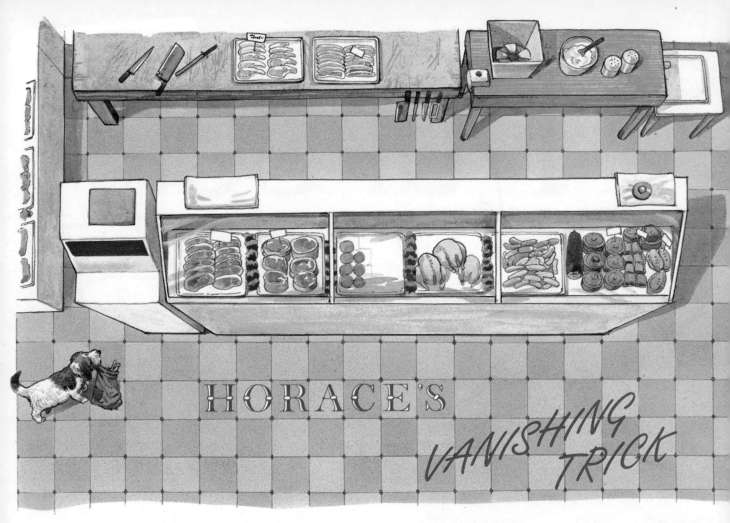

HORACE'S VANISHING TRICK

Horace was a dog. He had no collar and he had no home. And worst of all, he had no food. He wandered from dustbin to dustbin, searching for scraps of food. Wherever Horace went, he carried a large, tattered bag full of dry bones. When he could find nothing better, he would munch sadly on a dry bone, trying to imagine it was a big, juicy steak.

One gloomy Monday, Horace was sniffing round when he saw the open door of a butcher's shop. A delicious smell was coming from inside. Horace crept to the door and looked in. There was no-one in sight.

"Ho, ho!" he said to himself, licking his lips.

He padded silently into the shop, and just happened to find a large tray of bacon.

"Hmm, delicious!" said Horace when the tray was empty.

Then he just happened to find a large tray of chops.

"Hmmm, delicious!" said Horace when the tray was quite empty. He was looking about for more, when suddenly he heard footsteps. Quick as a flash,

he slid beneath the sausage-making machine.

Mr Joint the butcher walked into his shop and stopped short. Something was missing! "I thought I sliced a tray of bacon." Horace snuffled quietly to himself.

Then Mr Joint saw the second empty tray. "I'm sure I cut some chops, but I can't have done. Oh well, I'd better get on with the sausages." Horace sniggered to himself.

Mr Joint switched on the sausage-making machine, and put some pork into it. Round went the pork, whizzing past Horace's hungry nose. It came out at the other end as a string of sausages. Mr Joint put in some more pork. Just as it went past Horace's nose, he grabbed it and gulped it down. "Hmmm, delicious!"

Mr Joint waited for the sausages to come out. "That's strange." He put in more pork. Horace ate that, too. "This is ridiculous!" said Mr Joint, putting in

more pork. Horace gobbled that up as well.

Mr Joint eyed his machine suspiciously. "If the next lot doesn't come out, I'll have to investigate."

"Oh dear," thought Horace. "If he investigates, he'll find me, and I shan't have any more to eat. And I'm *so* hungry!" Then he had an idea. "Of course!"

"It's crazy!" cried Mr Joint. "I-I must be seeing things! Am I mad?" Under the machine, Horace tried to stifle his giggles, and spluttered into his shaggy paws.

"Do I hear somebody laughing?" asked Mr Joint angrily. He peered under the machine. There was Horace, gazing back, with a guilty expression on his face. "And who are you?"

"I'm Horace. I'm a dog."

"I can see that. What do you think you're doing under my sausage-making machine?"

Horace blushed. "Well, er, you see, um, I'm a meat-tester."

"A meat-tester?"

"Yes. I test meat. I eat it to see if it's all right. Your meat's all right. Very nice, in fact. Good enough to sell."

"But you've eaten it all!" wailed the butcher. "How can I sell it if you've scoffed it all?"

"I had to test it, didn't I? You can't sell it unless it's tested."

Mr Joint sighed. "I suppose you've *tested* my bacon, as well?"

"Oh yes. Very good indeed. But, um, cut the slices thicker next time."

Mr Joint put some more pork into the machine. As it passed by, Horace quickly ate it, and pushed in a dirty old bone! Out it came — as a bone sausage.

Mr Joint stared in amazement, while Horace giggled quietly to himself. In went another piece of pork. Out came another bone. In went the meat. Out came a bone.

Horace pretended to look under the machine, and fiddled with some screws. At last he reappeared smiling. "That should do the trick. Try it now."

Mr Joint put some pork into the machine and waited at the other end. Out came the sausages, ready to sell. He put in more pork, and out it came as sausages. "I don't know what you did, but my machine works better than ever!" He reached down and patted Horace — and suddenly felt how thin the dog was. "Why, you poor thing. I can count all the bones in your body. No wonder you ate my mince. Come and have some more."

The astonished Horace was offered plates of steak and kidney and liver. He stuffed himself silly, while Mr Joint watched.

In fact, Mr Joint decided that he liked Horace so very much that he invited Horace to stay. And that is exactly what Horace did. Now Mr Joint always cuts his bacon into much thicker slices than he did before.

Mr Joint was turning a deep purple. "You thief! Meat-stealer! Bacon-snatcher!"

Horace crouched under the machine. And when the butcher finally ran out of names to call him, Horace quietly said, "I can mend your machine for you."

"What do you know about my machine?"

"Throwing out old bones, isn't it? That's bad. Still, I might be able to help."

THE RUNAWAY PIANO

There were so many things in Mr Dick's junk shop that he had quite forgotten what some of them were. There were tables with funny legs, chairs with wobbly backs, beds with broken springs and all kinds of other useless items.

"What a muddle!" Mrs Dick would grumble. "Why don't you get rid of some of it?"

"Yes, yes, all right my dear, I will," Mr Dick would murmur. But he never did.

Tucked away in a dark and dusty corner, behind the shop door, was an old piano. It had once belonged to a famous pianist and its name had been written across the front in gleaming gold letters: 'Trumpelmetzel'. But over the years the lettering had faded until only the word 'Trumpel' remained.

There was no-one to play Trumpel now — only Grey-Whisker Mouse, who ran over the keys at night-time. And there was no-one to listen to Trumpel's music either — except for Jumbo, the white wooden elephant with only one tusk, who stood near the piano in the dark corner. He loved to hear the sounds that Trumpel made when Grey-Whisker Mouse ran over the keys.

"What wonderful music," he would say. "Please Trumpel, let's have that tune again."

One day when Mrs Dick was in the shop, she scolded Mr Dick yet again.

"It's about time you turned out all this rubbish. That old piano should be chopped up for firewood. And as for that dreadful white elephant — just look at it, it's only got one tusk."

"I suppose you're right, my dear," sighed Mr Dick. "Nobody seems to want things like that nowadays. I'll see about it tomorrow."

That night, when the pale moonbeams were shining into Mr Dick's shop, Grey-Whisker Mouse came out to scamper over the piano's ivory keys. But the piano played a very sad tune.

"What's wrong, Trumpel?" asked Grey-Whisker Mouse.

"Didn't you hear what Mr Dick said?" wailed Trumpel. "I'm going to be chopped up for firewood tomorrow."

"Why don't you run away?"

"How can I?" cried the piano. "I may have legs but I can't move them."

"I wish I could help," boomed Jumbo. "Real elephants are so strong. If only I could move!"

A blue moon had risen in the sky and was shining full on the white

elephant. And in the magic moonlight something very wonderful happened.

"Look! Look at Jumbo! He moved! I'm sure he moved!" squeaked Grey-Whisker Mouse excitedly.

"Yes," boomed Jumbo, "but I'll have to act fast. This kind of magic only happens once in a blue moon and doesn't last long."

The piano started to move, slowly at first, then faster and faster and faster until with a tremendous crash it burst through the doorway and landed out in the street.

"Oh no," groaned Trumpel. "Now you've done it, Jumbo. You'd better escape while you can."

9

At that very moment the moon disappeared behind a cloud. "Oh dear," said Jumbo. "I knew this magic wouldn't last. I can't move at all now."

Lights came on in the shops and houses round about, and soon people were running up the street. Mr Dick rushed downstairs to see what had happened. "How *did* the piano get there?" he said, rubbing his eyes. "*And* that elephant!" With a neighbour's help, Mr Dick carried the piano and the elephant back into the shop. Then, still feeling very puzzled, he went to bed.

Next morning, the story of the night's strange happenings soon spread through the town. One neighbour told another that Mr Dick's shop had been broken into — and someone else suggested that he must have some really priceless antiques. When Mrs Dick heard this suggestion, she said, "Oh yes, he has, oh of course he has. He has lots of priceless antiques."

After that, people began coming to the shop, first in ones and twos, then in threes and fours, eager to have the pick of Mr Dick's priceless antiques. Soon there was almost nothing left for Mr Dick to throw out *or* chop up. But still no-one seemed to want the old piano or the white wooden elephant with only one tusk.

Mr Dick was just about to close his shop at dinner-time when a young man

rushed in, clanging the doorbell.

"What can I do for you, young sir?" asked Mr Dick. He recognised the young man as a music student who lived in a tiny little room down the street.

"I heard you have a piano for sale," said the young man. "Is it still here? Can I see it?"

"Mr Dick will let you have it cheap," said Mrs Dick hastily, "*if* you take that elephant as well."

The young man hesitated. He was not sure that he had room for an elephant as well as a piano. He ran his fingers thoughtfully over Trumpel's keys. "I do like the sound it makes." Then he looked at the white elephant. "All right. The elephant goes with the piano. I'll take them both."

Jumbo was so happy — and so was Trumpel! And inside the piano Grey-Whisker Mouse did a little dance of joy — for he had no intention of being left behind by his two friends.

"You won't regret it, young man," said Mr Dick. "This piano used to belong to a famous pianist. So I'm sure that with its help you too will be famous one day!"

And do you know — he was!

11

COUNTING CHICKENS

Rashid the beggar and Fatima his wife lived in an upturned cart near the city wall. The cart was their only possession, they were so poor! So every day Rashid left Fatima to guard the home, while he went off to beg for food.

One very hot day, Rashid was walking along gloomily with his head cast down. And there, by the roadside, half-hidden in the grass, he found a big, brown, speckled chicken's egg.

Rashid rushed home in delight and showed the egg to Fatima. "Look, look! Our luck's changed! If I can hatch out this egg, I'll have a chicken of my own!"

His wife was so thrilled, she threw her arms round him. "Eggs every day!"

"Dozens!" shouted Rashid. "And some of those eggs will hatch into chickens, too! We'll have roast chicken every week and still have plenty to sell in the market!"

"Enough money to buy a cow one day. And the cow will produce gallons of milk — then we can buy a bull, and breed more cattle."

Fatima began to dance round the cart. "We'll be rich, rich, rich!"

Rashid stood up straight and tall.

"Before the year is out, I'll be the richest cattle dealer north of the Sahara. Sheiks and merchants will ride hundreds of miles to buy cows from me — and eggs and chickens."

Fatima put her hands to her mouth in amazement. "Could we ever be rich enough for me to have a *new dress?*"

"Dress? You'll have a thousand dresses, and embroidered slippers to match! You'll be carried everywhere by servants! And I'll own fifty racing camels and build a palace with a thousand rooms!"

Fatima was puzzled. "Why will we need a thousand rooms? They'll be awfully hard to keep clean."

"For the servants, of course!"

"Of course! The servants!"

"And the dancing girls! I'll have a troop of dancing girls to dance for me every night — and at least a dozen beautiful young wives to care for me in my old age. Oh yes, I can see them now, wiping my brow with rosewater, fetching me glasses of sherbet, feeding me

grapes, stroking my br . . . Ow!"

Fatima had snatched the large, brown, speckled chicken's egg and smashed it on Rashid's head.

The yolk trickled down his face, the eggshell glistened in his hair. "Dancing girls, indeed!" his wife bawled. "Beautiful young wives! Ha!" And she stalked off to sit under the cart and sulk.

Which only goes to prove that *you should never count your chickens before they are hatched.*

14

The Birthday Candle

It was Sharon's sixth birthday. She had a red scarf and a doll, a pair of roller skates, and a big cake with six candles on it. It was a white cake, with flowers made of blue icing. Sharon's mum lit the candles. "Now, blow them all out," she said.

Sharon blew very hard, and four candles went out. She took another breath and blew again. One more candle went out. There was one left shining by itself. It was a *very* bright candle. Sharon took a deep breath and blew. The flame wobbled, but it did not go out. Sharon blew and blew, but still the candle would not go out.

Her mother got cross. "I'll do it." But though she blew and blew, the candle went on shining. Sharon took it to Dad.

He blew so hard that the veins stood out on his forehead, but the candle would not go out. He took it into the kitchen and poured water over it. It spluttered hot wax on his fingers, but it did not go out. Now Sharon's dad was cross. He threw the candle out of the window. It bounced on the head of a policeman passing by.

"Hey! Who's throwing candles?" shouted the policeman.

"I'm sorry," said Sharon coming out of the house. "But it won't go out."

"Won't go out? Don't be silly." He put the candle under his big boot and stamped on it. The flame burned a hole in his sole! The policeman was angry, and threw the candle as far as he could.

it up, and sat down to think what to do next.

A passing fire-engine squealed to a halt. The firemen turned their hoses on the fire. Sharon was soaked to the skin, but the candle still shone!

"How amazing!" exclaimed the firemen. But Sharon had gone. She was on her way to the sea.

Soon she stood on a cliff-top looking out over the cold, wet sea. She threw her candle over the edge. It fell far away, down below, amongst the foaming waves.

. Sharon ran after it. The candle rolled into a shop and the manager picked it up and blew on it. "It won't go out," said Sharon.

"Don't worry. I'll soon solve that." The manager put the candle in a small tin box and shut it up tight. "Candles need air to burn," he explained. Then he wrapped up the tin, wrote 'To the Fire Brigade' on the label, and posted the parcel in the post box. "There! That'll fix it!" he said.

Just then the post box exploded and burst into flames. Letters were scattered around Sharon's feet. In amongst them lay her birthday candle, still shining. She picked

The sea gathered round the little candle and hurled it high in the air. It landed at Sharon's feet, still burning. She smiled. She did not really want her candle to go out now. She decided to take it home.

But as she set off, there was a swirling sound, and a large furry paw rested on her shoulder. Long claws dug into her skin. A huge hound, with purple wings, was standing behind her. "Where have you been?" it demanded. "I've been searching for you everywhere."

"Wh-who are you?" asked Sharon.

"I'm the trusty hound of the Man-in-the-Moon, and I've come for the star. You should have given it to me hours ago! The whole universe is waiting! It's not every day a new star is born, you know."

"Star?" said Sharon. "What star?"

"Why, that star, of course," barked the Moon-hound. "Don't you know a star when you see one? How it got on to your birthday cake I don't know!" He seized the candle and flew up into the sky, higher and higher, until Sharon could not see him any more.

But that night, when all the stars came out, there was an extra one in the sky.

"What happened to that candle that wouldn't go out?" asked Sharon's mum.

"It's up there," said Sharon, pointing to the bright speck in the sky.

Mum shook her head. "Silly girl," she murmured.

But it was the best birthday present Sharon had ever had. And it is still there now.

It just won't go out!

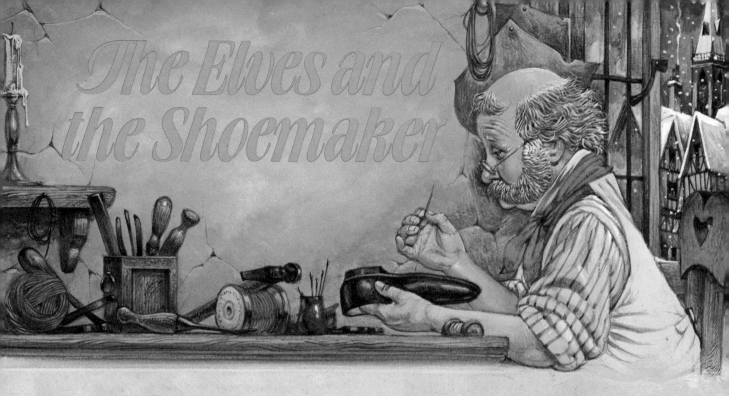

The Elves and the Shoemaker

"Can't you work any faster, my dear?" said the shoemaker's wife anxiously.

The shoemaker smiled: "Oh. I *could* work faster," he said. "I could cut out the leather for my shoes less neatly, and I could sew with bigger stitches. But I like to give the customers my very best workmanship. And that takes time."

"I know, dear, but there's no money left over to buy more leather. You work so carefully that it takes you two days to make one pair of shoes."

"I'm doing my best," said the shoemaker sadly. "My eyesight isn't as good as it was and my fingers aren't so quick."

The shoemaker continued to do his slow, careful best. But there was soon no money left to buy leather, and all his hides and suedes were used up. Only one scrap of leather was left on his workbench.

"What shall we do tomorrow when there's no leather to sew and when there are no more shoes to sell?" asked his wife.

The shoemaker smiled. "Well, let's worry about that tomorrow".

He spent all day cutting out a pair of shoes from the last of the leather. "These are probably the last shoes I shall ever make," he thought, "so they must be my best."

When he went to bed, he left the cut-out shapes on his workbench.

"I'm sorry we are so poor, my dear," he said to his wife as he climbed into bed.

"You can only do your best," she said comfortingly. "You can't do any more."

In the morning, the shoemaker cleaned his glasses and threaded his needle and looked around for the pieces of leather. But something *amazing* had happened. A finished pair of shoes stood in the centre of the bench, perfect to the last shiny buckle. Someone had made the shoes for him, overnight.

"Just look at the workmanship!" he exclaimed, showing them to his wife. "And look at the beautiful tiny stitches! Who could have made them?"

The shoes were so well made that they sold for twice the usual price. So the old shoemaker was able to buy a new strip of leather and cut out *two* pairs of shoes during the day. At night he left the cut-out shapes on his workbench and went to bed a much more cheerful man.

In the morning, the two pairs of shoes were completely finished, right down to the tags on their laces.

"What craftsmanship!" said the shoemaker to his wife. The shoes brought such a good price that this time he was able to buy enough leather for *four* pairs of shoes. And the next night, the mysterious visitors sewed all four pairs.

"Such perfect cobbling!" exclaimed the customers. And they came from miles around to buy the shoemaker's wares. There were long, glossy riding boots for the men and pretty velvet dancing shoes for the ladies.

"We have enough leather for a lifetime!" said the shoemaker's happy wife. "And so many people come here to buy their shoes that we are almost *rich*!"

But the shoemaker was thinking. "Wouldn't you like to know who is helping us every night? It's time we found out."

So one cold night, just before Christmas, the shoemaker left the cut-out leather on his workbench, then he and his wife hid nearby.

As midnight struck, out from behind the clock crept six naked little elves. They climbed on to the bench and went to work at once, sewing and hammering

and lacing and polishing. Every now and then they stopped to blow into their cold hands or stamp their cold feet or hug themselves against the chilly night air. They were shivering blue from head to foot.

"Poor little mites," said the shoemaker's wife. "All that work for us and they haven't got a shirt or even a pair of boots."

"Well, after all they've done for us, we ought to give them a thank-you present," said the shoemaker.

The next day his wife was soon busy cutting out little shirts and trousers from some bright warm cloth. The shoemaker took out his finest needle and softest leather and made a handsome pair of boots for each elf.

On Christmas night, they left their presents on the workbench and hid as they had done before. It was bitterly cold. When the six little elves appeared, they were shuddering and shivering, and their breath turned white in the frosty air.

They were confused at first, when they could find no boot leather to sew. But when they saw the clothes and realised that they were for them, they put them on and danced about, laughing and clapping their hands inside their new woolly mittens.

"No more cobbling for us! We're smart fellows now!" And they all sang as they danced out of the shop and down the street.

"So! No more help from the elves," said the shoemaker's wife, laughing. "How will you manage now that so many people come to you for their shoes and boots?"

The shoemaker smiled. "I'll just have to do my best," he said.

"I'm sure you will, my dear," said his wife. "You always do."

THE BOY WHO CRIED "WOLF"

Once there was a shepherd boy who looked after the sheep for all the people in his village. Some days it was pleasant in the hills and the time seemed to pass quickly. On the other days the boy grew bored and restless — there was nothing to do but watch the sheep nibbling at the grass from morning till night.

One day he decided to amuse himself, and he walked to the top of a crag above the village. "Help! Wolf!" he shouted at the top of his voice. "A wolf is eating the sheep!"

The moment the villagers heard the shepherd boy shouting they rushed out of their houses and up the hill to help him drive the wolf away . . . and found him laughing his head off at the trick he'd played on them. Angrily, they returned home, and the boy, still giggling, went back to watching the sheep.

A week or so later, the boy became bored again and walked to the top of the crag and shouted: "Help! Wolf! A wolf is eating the sheep!" Once again, the villagers rushed up the hill to help him. Once again, they found him laughing at their red faces and were very angry, but

there was nothing they could do except scold him.

Three weeks later the boy played exactly the same trick, and again a month after that, and yet again a few weeks after that. "Help! Wolf!" he would cry. "A wolf is eating the sheep!" Every time, the villagers dashed up the hill to help him, and every time they were met with the sight of the shepherd boy falling about with laughter over the trick he'd played on them.

Then, late one winter evening, as the boy was gathering the sheep to take them home, a wolf really *did* come prowling around the flock.

The shepherd boy was very scared. The wolf looked huge in the fading light and the boy had only his crook to fight with. He raced to the crag, yelling: "Help! Wolf! A wolf is eating the sheep!" But none of the villagers came to help the boy, for nobody believes a liar, even when he tells the truth.

"He's played that silly trick once too often," they all said. "If there *is* a wolf, then it will just have to eat the boy this time." And it did.

DEP. LEG. B-18.471-98